EDGE BOOKS™

DRAGONS

# DRAGON LEGENDS

*by Matt Doeden*

*Consultant*
Dr. Peter Hogarth
Professor, Department of Biology
University of York, United Kingdom

Capstone *press*®

Mankato, Minnesota

Edge Books are published by Capstone Press,
151 Good Counsel Drive, P.O. Box 669, Mankato, Minnesota 56002.
www.capstonepress.com

*Library of Congress Cataloging-in-Publication Data*
Doeden, Matt.
 Dragon legends / by Matt Doeden.
  p. cm. — (Edge books. Dragons)
  Summary: "Describes popular dragon legends and myths from around
the world" — Provided by publisher.
  Includes bibliographical references and index.
  ISBN–13: 978-1-4296-1294-4 (hardcover)
  ISBN–10: 1-4296-1294-0 (hardcover)
  1. Dragons — Juvenile literature. I. Title. II. Series.
GR830.D7D63 2008
398'.469 — dc22                                    2007025093

**Editorial Credits**
Aaron Sautter, editor; Ted Williams, designer; Richard Pellegrino and
  Tod Smith, illustrators; Krista Ward, colorist; Jo Miller, photo researcher

**Photo Credits**
Alamy/rochaphoto, 17
Art Resource, N.Y./Eric Lessing, 26; Werner Forman, 22
The Granger Collection, New York, 21, 28
The Kobal Collection/20th Century Fox, 29 (bottom)
Mary Evans Picture Library, 13, 19, 24–25; Arthur Rackham, 14
Shutterstock/abzora, backgrounds; Andrey Zyk, backgrounds
Supplied by Capital Pictures, 29 (top)

1 2 3 4 5 6 13 12 11 10 09 08

# TABLE OF CONTENTS

## CHAPTER ONE

# BEOWULF AND THE DRAGON

The kingdom of Geatland was under attack. A mighty dragon terrorized the countryside. It burned villages and farms and killed many people. Only Beowulf, the nation's mighty king and hero, could stop the dragon.

Beowulf's soldiers trembled in fear as they approached the dragon's **lair**. When the dragon burst from its cave, most of the men fled in terror. Only one brave and loyal warrior, Wiglaf, stayed to help his king.

**lair** – a place where a wild animal lives and sleeps

Beowulf wouldn't turn back. His kingdom needed him. With a shout, Beowulf charged at the dragon. It was a brutal fight, but with Wiglaf's help, Beowulf finally killed the monster. But Beowulf was hurt in the fight. He staggered back as blood gushed from his neck. The dragon had bitten him! The dragon's fiery venom flowed through his body. Gasping for air, Beowulf fell to the ground. The kingdom was safe, but the king was dead.

## Beasts of Legend

History is filled with stories about dragons. The ancient poem *Beowulf* is just one of them. Every culture in the world has fantastic tales about powerful dragons. In stories from Europe and other Western countries, dragons are seen as terrifying beasts. But in Asian tales, dragons are usually peaceful and friendly to people. Wherever the stories come from, tales about dragons have captured our imaginations for hundreds of years.

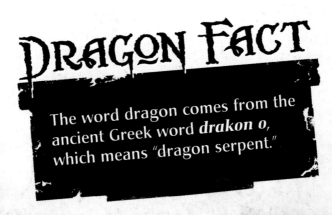

# DRAGON FACT

The word dragon comes from the ancient Greek word *drakon o*, which means "dragon serpent."

## Chapter Two

# Western Dragon Legends

Many Western legends tell about the struggle between people and dragons. Dozens of stories are filled with deadly dragons and the brave warriors who fought them.

## Saint George and the Dragon

Perhaps the most famous of all dragon legends tells the story of a dragon that terrorized the town of Silene, Libya. The dragon demanded that the people give up their sheep for it to eat. If they didn't, the dragon would attack the town every night. The fearful townspeople did all they could to keep the dragon satisfied. But they soon ran out of sheep.

The dragon then demanded they give up their children. A **lottery** was created to decide which child would be sent to the dragon each day. Soon, the king's daughter was chosen. The king begged for her life to be spared. But the villagers had already given up many of their own children. They felt the king's daughter had been chosen fairly.

The princess was tied up and left near the dragon's lair. But just as the dragon began moving toward the princess, a soldier named Saint George rode to her rescue. George charged toward the beast and pierced its tough skin with his long, sharp **lance**. Then he finished killing the monster with his sword. Silene was safe. To honor Saint George, the grateful king built a church at the very spot the dragon died.

**lottery** – a way of randomly choosing someone
**lance** – a long spear used by soldiers on horseback

# The Lambton Worm

Another famous dragon legend comes from England. According to the story, young John Lambton skipped church one Sunday to go fishing. But all he caught was a large, scaly worm. Disgusted, John tossed the ugly worm down a well and forgot about it.

But the worm lived and grew in the well. In a few years, it had grown into a powerful dragon. The dragon terrorized the countryside, eating sheep and threatening everyone in its path.

During this time, John had left home to fight in a war. When he returned, he learned what the dragon was doing to his homeland. He knew it was his fault. John went to a wise old woman for advice. She told him he could kill the monster, but only if he wore special armor with long spikes attached to it. He also had to kill the very next living thing he saw after the dragon was dead. If he didn't, his family would be cursed.

John promised to do as the woman said. After a great battle, the dragon was dead. John blew his horn to signal his father to release a dog that he was holding nearby. John planned to kill the dog to keep his promise. But John's father forgot the plan. Excited by his son's victory, he rushed to John's side instead of sending the dog. John couldn't kill his own father. Because John broke his promise, the Lambton family was cursed with bad luck for the next nine generations.

# Sigurd and Fafnir

Another popular Western dragon legend comes from Scandinavia in northern Europe. In this story, a young man named Sigurd was the orphaned son of a great warrior. Raised by the dwarf Regin, Sigurd grew up strong and proud.

Years before, Regin and his brother, Fafnir, killed their father to steal his treasure. But Fafnir betrayed Regin and took the treasure for himself. Then Fafnir turned himself into a mighty dragon to defend it. One day, Regin asked Sigurd to kill Fafnir so they could share the treasure.

Sigurd had a powerful sword named Gram. With Gram in hand, Sigurd hid in a hole near Fafnir's lair and waited for the beast. As Fafnir passed over the hole, Sigurd thrust Gram into Fafnir's belly. It was a killing blow. The dying dragon's blood rained down over Sigurd.

The magic in Fafnir's blood changed Sigurd. He became stronger and faster. His skin became as tough as a dragon's hide. No weapon could pierce him. Sigurd also understood the speech of birds. Two birds had overheard Regin's original plan. They told Sigurd that Regin planned to kill him to keep the treasure for himself. Angered, Sigurd killed Regin instead and claimed the dragon's treasure as his reward.

## Chapter Three

# Eastern Dragon Legends

Dragons in Eastern legends are similar to Western dragons in many ways. They are powerful creatures that can fly or perform magic. But there are also important differences. Asian dragons are rarely shown as beasts to be feared. Instead, they are respected for their power and wisdom.

## The Four Dragons

One legend from China tells of four dragons that lived in the Eastern Sea. They were known as the Black Dragon, the Long Dragon, the Pearl Dragon, and the Yellow Dragon. According to the tale, China once did not have any rivers. People depended on rain to grow their crops. One year, a terrible drought took hold of the land. The people were suffering and starving. The four dragons decided to help the people. They scooped water out of the sea and sprayed it into the sky. It fell down as rain and saved the people's crops.

But the god of the sea was furious with the four dragons. They took water from the ocean without his permission. The angry sea god told China's emperor what the dragons had done. The emperor punished the dragons by imprisoning them under four mountains. But the dragons still wanted to help the people. They turned themselves into four rivers to keep bringing people the water they needed. According to the legend, this is how China received its four great rivers — the Black River, the Long River, the Pearl River, and the Yellow River.

*In many Chinese legends, dragons like helping people.*

# The Dragon's Pearl

Another story from China shows the power of a dragon's pearl. One day, young Tchang went to find the Great God of the West. He wanted to ask why he and his mother were so poor. On his way, he met a woman and her daughter. "Please ask the god why my daughter won't talk," the woman begged. Next, he met an old man. "Please ask the god why my trees bear no fruit," the old man said. Finally, Tchang met a dragon. "Please ask the god why I cannot fly," it begged him. Tchang agreed to each of their requests.

Finally, Tchang found the Great God. The god said he would answer only three questions. Tchang kept his promise to those he had met on his journey. He asked the god their questions instead of his own. Then he returned the way he had come.

"The Great God says that to fly, you must first do a good deed," he told the dragon. Grateful for his help, the dragon gave Tchang his most precious possession — a magic pearl. Immediately, the dragon flew up into the sky. Next, Tchang used the magic pearl to show the old man how to make his trees grow fruit. Finally, he met the woman and her daughter. He touched the girl's lips with the pearl, and she could speak once again. Tchang and the girl fell in love and got married.

At home, Tchang found his mother had gone blind from crying. But when he gave her the dragon's pearl, her sight returned. The magic pearl brought fish to a nearby lake and helped the crops grow on the land. With the precious pearl, Tchang, his new wife, and his mother happily lived out their days.

# Dragon Fact

Vietnamese myths tell of a dragon named Lac Long Quan who married a fairy named Au Co. Their children became the first Vietnamese people.

*Eastern dragons are often shown carrying large magic pearls.*

# DRAGON FACT

It is thought that the story of Tiamat and Marduk was first told around the year 2000 BC. It is one of the oldest dragon legends in the world.

CHAPTER FOUR

# Other Dragon Legends

Dragons aren't just found in the legends of the West or Asia. From ancient Egypt to Central America, dragons live in the myths and stories of cultures all over the world.

## The Legend of Tiamat

According to an ancient myth from the Middle East, two gods represented the different parts of the earth. Apsu was the male god of fresh water and the **abyss**. Tiamat was the female dragon god of saltwater and **chaos**. Tiamat had hard scales, feathered wings, and the head of a lion. Her body was so strong and tough that no weapon could pierce it.

> **abyss** – a place where nothing exists
> **chaos** – total confusion

Tiamat and Apsu had many children who later became the gods of the world. But their children behaved badly. Apsu wanted to kill his children as punishment. But they killed Apsu instead. Tiamat was overwhelmed with grief. The myth says the Tigris and Euphrates rivers were formed from her tears.

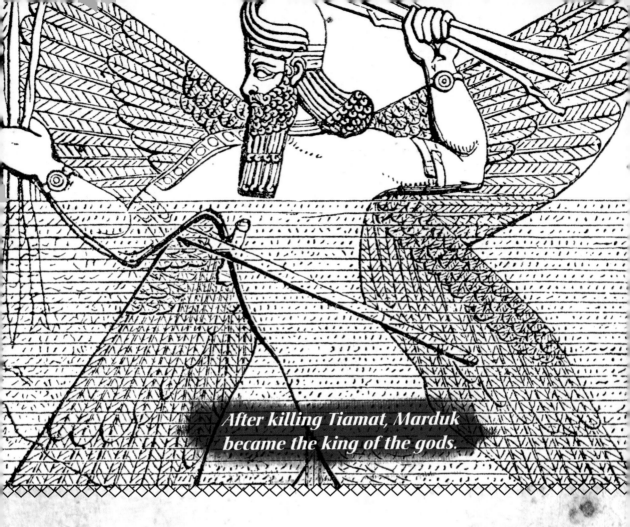

*After killing Tiamat, Marduk became the king of the gods.*

Tiamat soon planned her revenge for Apsu's death. But Marduk, one of Tiamat's grandchildren, attacked her before she could carry out her plan. Marduk shot an arrow through Tiamat's mouth. The arrow split her heart in two. Marduk then divided Tiamat's body into two parts to create the sky and the land. The myth says Marduk also created humans to serve the gods as slaves.

*The serpent Apep (bottom) is almost always defeated by Ra in Egyptian art.*

# Apep

In stories from Egypt, Apep was the god of darkness and death. Apep was often shown as a fearsome serpent with a head made of stone. Apep was the enemy of the Egyptian sun god, Ra.

Apep was jealous of Ra and his power. Every night, when Ra entered the underworld, Apep would attack. The great dragon tried to use magic to put Ra and his followers to sleep. But Ra and his protectors usually overcame Apep. There were times when Apep won the battle, though. The Egyptians believed that Apep's attacks caused earthquakes, storms, and other disasters. One story says that Apep sometimes swallowed Ra whole, which caused **solar eclipses**.

**solar eclipse** – when the moon passes in front of the sun

## DRAGON FACT

Ancient natives of Central America worshipped a dragon god named Quetzalcoatl. His name means "feathered snake."

## Dragons All Around

The stories in this book are just a few of the dragon legends found around the world. Other legendary creatures like unicorns, trolls, and fairies have lived in our stories for hundreds of years. But none of them are as popular as dragons. Among imaginary beasts, the dragon is truly king.

## Today's Dragons

Today, dragons are found everywhere from books and movies to video games. Much of the current dragon craze can be traced back to author J. R. R. Tolkien. Tolkien's stories are filled with many strange creatures like orcs, trolls, and dragons. In *The Hobbit,* a small, humanlike creature called a hobbit helps defeat a fearsome dragon named Smaug.

Today's dragons keep people entertained in many ways. They are a big part of the role-playing game *Dungeons & Dragons.* Many are seen in movies like *Eragon* and the *Harry Potter* series. Dragons also appear in several video games. And they continue to be featured in many fantasy books. Though they aren't real, dragons continue to capture people's imaginations.

# Glossary

**abyss** (uh-BISS) — a dark, empty place where nothing exists

**chaos** (KAY-oss) — total confusion

**lair** (LAIR) — a place where a wild animal lives and sleeps

**lance** (LANSS) — a long spear used by soldiers on horseback

**lottery** (LOT-ur-ee) — a way of randomly choosing someone to win a prize or participate in an event

**myth** (MITH) — a story told by people in ancient times; myths often try to explain natural events.

**solar eclipse** (SOH-lur i-KLIPS) — a period of daytime darkness when the moon passes between the sun and earth

**venom** (VEH-nuhm) — a poisonous liquid that is injected into prey

# Read More

**Brucken, Kelli M.** *Dragons*. Mysterious Encounters. San Diego: KidHaven Press, 2006.

**Krensky, Stephen.** *Dragons*. Monster Chronicles. Minneapolis: Lerner, 2007.

**Penner, Lucille Recht.** *Dragons*. New York: Random House, 2004.

# Internet Sites

FactHound offers a safe, fun way to find Internet sites related to this book. All of the sites on FactHound have been researched by our staff.

Here's how:
1. Visit *www.facthound.com*
2. Choose your grade level.
3. Type in this book ID **1429612940** for age-appropriate sites. You may also browse subjects by clicking on letters, or by clicking on pictures and words.
4. Click on the **Fetch It** button.

**FactHound will fetch the best sites for you!**

# Index